5

MINUTE

Magical Tales

bookoli

Published in 2020 by Bookoli,
12 Laura Place, Bath BA2 4BL.
Bookoli is an imprint of Curious Universe UK Ltd.
Copyright © 2020 Curious Universe UK Ltd.
www.curiousuniverse.co.uk

CONTENTS

The Not-so-Giant Giant

Stomp was a giant.

Just not as giant as the other giants.

He towered over humans, but other giants towered over him.

And they let him know it. They teased him and joked and laughed and were as mean as giants could be.

Stomp tried to show he was just as scary as they were.

He stomped hard to shake the ground.
But the others only stomped and shook harder.

He *ROARED* as loudly as he could.
But he didn't scare a single human away.

Then he sniffed a very big SNIFf ...

... and noticed
something peculiar.

"Humans!" Stomp cried out.

"Fee-fi-fo-fum,
I smell an
Englishman!"

The others laughed.
"With that tiny nose?
I doubt it, little Stomp."

Just then, they heard a loud **BANG**.

And again. **BANG**.

BANG! BANG! BANG!

"Someone's chopping!" a giant shouted.

"Humans!" someone else yelled. "Chopping down our beanstalk."

"What do we doooo?" they panicked.

The giants slid from side to side as their home tilted back and forth with every hit of the axe. They were so tall, they couldn't keep their balance.

But Stomp could. And he had an idea.

"Everybody stomp! Everybody roar!"

said Stomp. So the giants kicked their feet and roared loudly. For a short moment, the chopping stopped.

Stomp quickly tossed a vine down. He pulled the axe up out of the stunned chopper's hands. Then he wrapped the vine around the beanstalk to keep it steady.

"RUN AWAY!"

Stomp roared down.

It may not have been as loud as the other giants, but it was loud enough to scare the humans this time. They ran away, never to return again. Stomp had saved the giants!

"Hooray for Stomp!" shouted his friends. "The little giant with the BIG idea!"

And from that day on, the giants always went to Stomp if they needed a problem solving.

However big or small.

A Spell Gone Wrong

Far away, in a magical land of potions and spells, there lived a little family of wizards and witches.

"Look what I can do," said Wiz the witch. She waved her wand at a cauldron in the kitchen.

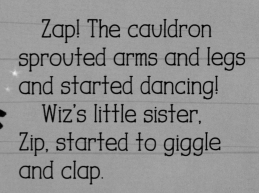

Zap! The cauldron sprouted arms and legs and started dancing! Wiz's little sister, Zip, started to giggle and clap.

"That's nothing," said their brother, Kaz.
"Watch what I can do." He waved his wand
in the air.

Zaaaap!

All at once, frogs fell down
from the ceiling. They lined
up on the table, burst into a
deep, croaky song and started
dancing around the kitchen.

Zip giggled again.

More, more,
more!

Wiz pointed her wand sharply at some herbs on the windowsill. Zap! The herbs grew up, up, up and shot out of the window in an instant.

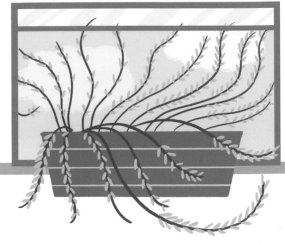

Zap! Zap!

Kaz pointed her wand at the cat, and it grew bigger and bigger and bigger, until its pointy ears touched the ceiling.

Wiz and Kaz were getting angry now, each trying to outdo the other.

Zip ducked as sparks flew all around the room.

Suddenly...

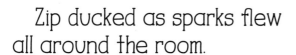

ZAP, ZAP, ZZZZZAAAAP!

Wiz and Kaz's magic collided in a big explosion.

BONG! BING! BONGGGGG!

The grandfather clock chimed an eerie tune as sparks hit its hands. Then everything went quiet.

More than that, everything stopped still.

Look what you did!

Look what YOU did!

The clock stopped tick-tocking, Zip stopped giggling, and the kitchen stopped singing and dancing. Nobody and nothing moved. Everything had frozen.

Except Wiz and Kaz. They looked at each other.

"Dad is going to be SO angry with us," said Wiz. "We froze the baby!"

The pair knew they had to act fast.

"I'll fix this," said Kaz. He waved his wand and said a spell,

**"Zip, zop, zap-attack,
Make everything go back!"**

A single mug fell to the ground with a clink that echoed loudly in the silent kitchen. The mug rattled as it rolled under the big, quiet clock.

But nothing else changed.

"So you can make things fall? Big help," said Wiz.
"Well, what can you do? Make them dance?" said Kaz.

Then his face lit up as an idea came to him.
"Actually, you do just that! And I'll make them fall.
And together, we'll put this kitchen back to normal."

Together, Wiz and Kaz magicked everything back into place. The mugs fell down, the frogs danced out of the kitchen, Zip danced back into life and the clock tick-tocked again.

"Not bad," smiled Kaz.   **"Again!"** clapped Zip.

"Wow, we can do some pretty cool magic together," said Wiz. "When we work together!"

Secrets in the Sky

Jack, Ben and Lily were racing through the woods behind Lily's house.

But just as the three giggled and ran ahead, the sky turned dark and rainclouds appeared.

A mix of raindrops and sunbeams broke through the leaves to the ground below.

The three friends dashed quickly to the big tree for cover.

And that's when they saw it. That very rare and special thing: the end of a rainbow.

It started at the tree's roots and stretched high into the sky, disappearing into the clouds.

Lily stepped forward.

19

She reached out and touched the rainbow gently. It was solid! She started climbing.

Jack and Ben followed close behind. Up and up they climbed, past squirrels in the trees and songbirds in the sky.

Come on!

The friends burst through the clouds and stood at the top of the glistening arch. A magical land in the clouds appeared below them.

20

"Wow," said Lily. "Our own secret sky world."
She ran off to explore.

Ben scooped up a handful of fluffy clouds.
"It tastes like candy!" he said.
Jack caught a raindrop on his tongue. "It tastes of strawberries and sweet lemons!" he said.

A sparkly, little rainbow fairy flew above their heads. "Welcome to our land in the sky. But remember, remember... when the rainbow starts to fade, it's time to go.

That is your only path back home!"

The friends played together in their secret world, jumping from cloud to cloud and tasting fluffy ice creams and rainbow candy canes.

As the sun started to lower in the sky, Ben noticed the rainbow was fading. "Look! It's time to go back home."

"Hang on ... where's Lily?" called Jack. But Lily was nowhere to be seen.

The friends skidded across the rainbow and squinted into the distance. All they could see were candy clouds and shimmering raindrops.

They couldn't see Lily anywhere, and the rainbow was fading ... fast.

Then up ahead, soaring on a bird, they spotted something...

"Lily!" they cried.

"I never want to leave," said Lily.

Ben and Jack quickly scooped her up, and they all whooshed down the rainbow, just in time.

As they ran back home in time for dinner, they all agreed ...

"We'll be back!"

The Dragon Problem

Far away, over the hills and beyond the trees, lies Fairy-tale Land. It is a land of princes, princesses and a few unicorns too.

It is beautiful, magical and peaceful.

Or, it was. Until the day the dragons came.

First, a small dragon flew in and landed right in the middle of Main Street.

Then, a great big one wandered into the bakery and ate up all the fairy cakes.

Then, another sat himself on the toilet when young princesses just had to go!

Soon, there were dragons EVERYWHERE.

The villagers were not happy.

They put up signs. But it turned out dragons can't read.

They tried to fight them. But they found out dragons are very strong!

They even sent in their scariest unicorns. But the dragons did not budge.

The people of Fairy-tale Land held a secret meeting. Everyone was invited, except for the dragons.

The castle hall filled up with villagers, princes, princesses, knights and unicorns. They all agreed that the dragons had to go.

That's when the dragons walked in.

It turned out that dragons have feelings too.

"You met without us?"
said the small dragon.

"Why didn't you just talk to us?"
said the big dragon

They were so upset about being left out of the meeting that they turned and flew away.

The villagers watched the
sky as the dragons disappeared into the clouds.

Suddenly, the clouds turned dark and ice began to fall.

An ice storm!

Storms like this came only once every hundred
years, but when they did, they meant trouble.

Look!

"My bakery!" shouted the baker.
"My flowers!" cried the florist.

"My house!" gasped the fairy.

The villagers looked at each other. Their town was slowly freezing over. They all knew there was only one thing to do. They needed help, and fast.

The unicorns dashed into the sky to find the dragons. The villagers waited nervously.

Finally, both the unicorns and dragons returned together.

"We're so sorry we tried to push you out," said a princess.

"Please, please help us!"

The dragons looked at each other and nodded. Then they breathed fire to melt the ice across the land. The villagers were over the moon. Their town had been saved, but they all felt bad for being so mean to the dragons.

"We were scared of you because you are different," said the princess. "But our kingdom needs friends that are different. Please stay and live here?"

"We would love to stay," said the dragons. After all, the dragons didn't like to hold a grudge.

And they all lived happily ever after. Expect, of course, when the dragons took way too long on the toilet.

Unicorn Dreams

Lila lived in a little cottage with her grandma,
on the edge of a forest. Every day, she loved to pick
flowers, climb trees and listen to the sounds of the birds.

But she longed for adventure.

She longed to share her world with a friend.

One day, a strange
sound echoed around the
forest.

Whoosh!
Fizz!
Crackle!

A gold star was glowing
on the ground.
"A wishing star!" Lila
gasped, slowly picking up
the fizzing star. She closed
her eyes tight.

"I wish...

I wish...

I wish for a friend to have adventures with!"

Up in the sky, clouds had started to swirl.
Glitter filled the forest, and a unicorn appeared
out of the trees.

"My name is Starlight," the unicorn smiled.
"I hope I haven't scared you."

But Lila wasn't scared at all. She was excited.

The wishing star had worked!

"I send stars when someone needs me," said Starlight.
"I am here to make your wish come true."

Lila clutched the star tightly and hopped
onto Starlight's back. In a flash, Starlight
soared into the clouds.

A rainbow shot across the sky.

As Lila reached out to touch it, her outfit transformed into a glittering rainbow cape.

"Now you are a rainbow princess," smiled Starlight.

Starlight flew higher, and higher, and higher ... until they reached an Ice Palace in the clouds. Snow fairies fluttered around excitedly when they saw Lila.

"Rainbow Princess!" the fairies giggled. They brought out marshmallow cakes and strawberry fizz. "Welcome to our home."

More fairies gathered around and performed a special dance, just for Lila.

Lila had never felt so happy!

She never wanted to leave her magical unicorn
friend in the sky. But it was soon time to go back home.
As she hugged Starlight tight, tears fell down her face.

"Don't be sad," Starlight smiled. "I'll always be here for
you. You just have to wish."

Starlight and Lila flew up into the starry night to put the wishing star back into the twinkling sky.

"This wishing star will always belong to you," said Starlight.

"Just look for the brightest star in the sky and make your wish."

Lila turned to Starlight and gave her the biggest hug. "Thank you, Starlight. For making my wish come true. I will never forget you."

Later that night, when Lila was back tucked up in her little cottage, she stared up at the night sky. Her star was twinkling bright, much brighter than all the other stars in the sky.

And from that moment, Lila knew she would never be lonely again. All she had to do was wish.

The Mermaid's Quest

Princess Fin sat on her throne, dreaming of adventure.

Her friends swam the big, wide sea and came back telling the most amazing tales. But Princess Fin was told to stay at home. She was too small, too young, too important.

If she was to be queen mermaid one day, she needed to stay safe.

One day, as Fin was sitting bored at home, she heard the elder mer-folk talking.

"Our home is in danger," they said.

"It's losing its light. We need the magical pearl to bring the light back."

Fin had heard tales of the magical pearl. It lay beyond the darkest depths of the ocean.

Without thinking, Fin leaped off her
throne and swam out into the sea.
She just had to help her kingdom and
have an adventure of her own.

A beautiful creature with a horn on its head
appeared out of the waves.
"Hello," said the creature. "Where are you going in
such a hurry?"

"Hello, narhwhal! I'm Fin," said Fin. "I'm on a quest to find the magical pearl and save my kingdom."

"Wow," said the narwhal. "I'm Nelly. I would love to have an adventure too!"

Fin was unsure of which way to swim. Nelly followed. "You look lost," he said.

"I'm not lost," said Fin, swimming around in circles. "But … where do I find the darkest depths of the ocean?"

Fin didn't want to admit it, but she was feeling nervous being alone in the big, wide sea.

"Follow me," said Nelly. "I can take you to the pearl and help to keep you safe."

"Oh, thank you!" said Fin. She was sure that together they would find the pearl safely.

Suddenly, Nelly shouted, "Watch out! In here! Quick!" Just in time, Fin and Nelly swam inside a shipwreck. as a shark slunk slowly past.

Nelly swam off again, and Fin followed.

They passed a seahorse who pointed them in the right direction.

They followed a busy school of fish.

They swam alongside the most majestic creature Fin had ever seen,

a great blue whale!

Finally, as they swam deeper, and deeper, they saw something sparkling.

A glowing, shimmering shell! Fin just knew it was what she was looking for.

She swam closer, and the shell opened slowly. It was as if it knew who she was. Fin reached carefully for the pearl and held it close.

Then she and Nelly rushed back through the sea. It was time to go back home.

We found it!

Fin barely recognized her kingdom when she returned. It was so dark and quiet.

But as she swam closer, the pearl began to glow brighter. It shone and shone, until suddenly, the whole kingdom was filled with twinkly lights and bursting with life once more.

Fin placed the pearl safely inside an open shell. The shell snapped closed and glowed gently.

"Fin!" Her parents rushed over to her. "You should never have left on your own!"

"I know, I'm sorry. But I wasn't on my own," Fin pointed at Nelly. **"And I just had to help."**

Her parents smiled. "Maybe you're more ready than we thought."

Fin smiled too. **She'd done it!**

She had saved her kingdom.

And best of all, she'd come home with a new friend and amazing tales to tell.